Andreas Bachmair
Madlen Make

Sarah doesn't want to be vaccinated

Illustrations by Alena Ryazanova
Translated by Kerry Giang-Davies

This book is not intended to provide any medical advice or to replace the treatment of a physician. The decision on whether to vaccinate your children or yourself is entirely up to you. I hope the information given in this book will help you to make an informed decision.

This book is dedicated to all children and parents who are concerned about vaccinations and refuse to give in to the constant vaccination propaganda.

Parents who refuse to vaccinate their children make this decision after careful consideration, because they are convinced that vaccinations do more harm than good. The decision not to vaccinate is often not an easy one, because one so often faces criticism and seems to be swimming upstream.

Dear parents, I hope this book will help you and your children to understand better the controversial issue of vaccination.

Sarah is sitting at the table having dinner with her parents and her little brother Tim. She is telling her parents all about the Girl and Boy Scout camp that she dearly wants to attend the following week and has brought home a long list from the Girl Scout troop. It lists everything she should bring with her to camp.

It also says that she should bring her vaccination record. "Mom, what's a vaccination record?" Sarah asks with surprise.
"A vaccination record lists all the vaccinations that you've received in your life. Vaccinations are shots that are supposed to protect you from getting sick. You and Tim don't have vaccination records though because you haven't been vaccinated." Her mother replied.

"Why aren't we vaccinated?" Sarah wonders with surprise. Her father replies, "People always tell you that vaccinations aren't dangerous but that's not true. A lot of people have gotten really sick from vaccination and that's why you're not vaccinated."

Sarah is really worried. She thinks she definitely needs a vaccination record so she can go to Scout camp. Her mother reassures her that she will call the troop leader in the morning and discuss the matter then. This makes Sarah feel a bit better about it.

Sarah and Tim's father takes them up to bed after dinner. They share a room.

He wanted to read them a bedtime story, but Tim insists on asking, "Daddy, is it bad that we aren't vaccinated?" His eyes hold concern, but his father answers, "You know, Tim, I wasn't vaccinated either, and I had all the childhood diseases."

"What is a childhood disease?" Sarah wants to know.

Her father explains, "It's a disease like, for example, measles. It used to be that most kids got measles and a few other diseases. That's why they're called childhood diseases. When you get measles, you get a high fever, a cough and lots of red dots on your body and have to stay in bed for two weeks."

"And then you get well again?" Tim asks curiously. "Yes, but it's really important that you don't lower the fever with medicines and that you drink lots of fluids. The fever is important so the body can actually fight the disease. Once you get over it, you're even healthier than you were before," their father replies.

The next day, Mom takes Sarah and Tim downtown. They buy a sleeping bag and a jackknife for her trip to Scout camp.

Sarah's mother calls the troop leader on her cell phone. He is very upset and can't understand why Sarah isn't vaccinated. He tells her that her daughter really needs to have a vaccination record for insurance purposes.

Sarah notices that something is wrong and asks her mother, "Mom, what did the troop leader say?"

"He said that he really needs a vaccination record from you," her mother explains.

Sarah is really worried that maybe she won't be able to go to camp after all and looks sadly at her new sleeping bag and the new jackknife. Her mother lays a calming hand on her shoulder and explains, "I'll send a letter with you for the troop leader. The letter will explain that you aren't vaccinated and are not to be vaccinated at camp either."

That takes a load off Sarah's mind and she hops around excitedly in a circle.

That weekend, Grandma Helen comes to visit them. She was one of the first Girl Scouts.

Grandma Helen takes the kids hiking in the woods and shows Sarah and Tim wonderful tricks. She can weave many blades of grass into knots that hold really well, but are easy to untie. She also knows signs for communicating in the forest without speaking a word. Then she makes a noise with her hands and her mouth that sounds like a real owl.

"Grandma, you're the best!" Sarah and Tim are impressed, because only Grandma Helen can do exciting things like that.

In the evening, the kids insist that Grandma Helen take them to bed and read them a story. They know that their grandma always tells really spooky stories that she heard in Scout camp back when she was a girl. They love the stories and always listen to her with wide-eyed excitement.

Later, the grown-ups sit in the living room and talk about vaccination. Sarah has secretly snuck out of her room and listens from the hallway to everything they say.

"No one can force you to vaccinate the children", Grandma Helen exclaims. "You have a vaccine exemption for them. Thank God, most of the states still have the legal right to opt out of using vaccines. Most people don't know this and are being scared into getting their kids vaccinated."

Grandma says to Dad, "You weren't vaccinated either. When you had measles, nobody got upset about it. Nowadays, when people have measles, everyone seems to think they have a terribly dangerous disease. People even say that only a vaccine can protect you from it."

Then Grandma explains why she didn't vaccinate Dad: her best friend's child became very sick after a vaccination. After that, Grandma didn't want to have anything to do with vaccinations.

Sarah is in class with Mrs. Potter, her math teacher. She chews on her pencil and thinks about what else she might need for Scout camp.

Suddenly, she realizes that she has no sleeping mat! She looks around at her classmates. Her gaze stops at her best friend Laura, who sits diagonally behind her. She remembers that Laura often goes camping with her parents and can surely lend her a sleeping mat. She quickly writes a short note, "Do you have a sleeping mat I can use?" and slips it secretly to Laura.

Laura reads the note and nods happily at Sarah. Luckily, she has an extra mat that Sarah can borrow. Now, hopefully, nothing else can get in the way of the exciting trip.

The bell rings and Mrs. Potter calls after the children, "Don't forget: the school doctor is coming tomorrow. All of you need to bring your vaccination records!"

Sarah and Tim are visiting Laura today. On Wednesdays, Sarah's mother works so the two of them always go over to Laura's house.

After lunch, Laura tells her mother that the school doctor is coming the next day so she needs to bring her vaccination record with her. "Yes, I already got it out for you, Sweetheart: it's with the other things for camp," Laura's mother replies.

"You see, Laura is vaccinated against everything," she adds, "so she won't get terrible diseases like measles."

Tim, who was listening the whole time, suddenly asks, "Is Max vaccinated, too?" Max is Laura's little brother. "Yes, he's also getting all his vaccinations," Laura's mother replies.

Sarah slides down a bit in her chair out of embarrassment and then says, "I'm not vaccinated. There's really bad stuff in vaccines and they can make you really sick. That's why my parents don't want me to be vaccinated."

Laura's mother stares at her in surprise and then mumbles, "Well, hopefully you'll never get sick!"

Sarah and Tim are waiting for Dad in the front yard, by the garage. Sarah's bicycle needs to be fixed before she can take it to Guide and Scout camp. She has already cleaned her bike and now Dad needs to adjust the brakes. They're not working quite right.

Dad puts his briefcase down and fetches the tool case from the garage. Then he adjusts the brakes and tells them that a well-functioning bicycle is like a healthy body. "When you give your body what it needs, it works just great."

Tim asks what he should give his body. "Good food, exercise and sunshine," their father winks at him. When he finishes adjusting the brakes, they go inside together.

In Sarah's room, Sarah's mother has already started packing her things for Scout camp. "Will all of that really fit into my backpack?" Sarah wonders. "That's a lot of stuff. I also brought a sleeping mat from Laura."

Together, Mom and Sarah go down the list of everything Sarah should take on the trip. "Other than the vaccination record, we have everything," Mom declares.

"Tomorrow, I'm supposed to bring my vaccination record to school; the school doctor is coming," Sarah tells her mother nervously. Mom gives her the letter that she had already prepared. The letter states that Sarah is not vaccinated and therefore has no vaccination record.

"If the school doctor has any questions, tell him to call me," Mom tells her.

Tim would also like to go to Scout camp. He draws a picture and hangs it up with Mom.

Then he explains to her excitedly what the wonderful thing he just drew is: "These are the tents and these are the kids playing 'Tag' with the dog. First the dog has to catch the kids and then the kids get to catch the dog. Also, in the forest, there are lots of nice sticks for the dog to play with. At night, when the kids are sleeping, the dog keeps watch so no wild animals can approach. I think I'll also draw a bonfire in the picture, then everyone can warm up if it gets too cold at night."

Mom chuckles. "And what's that?" she asks as she points to a yellow rectangle. "That's Laura's vaccination record, because she's taking it with her to camp," Tim explains.

The next day, the school doctor is doing check-ups in the gym. One after another, the children go in to see the doctor. Sarah comes out crying so Mrs. Potter runs over to comfort her.

"Sarah, whatever is the matter?" She asks in a concerned voice.

"The school doctor said I have to get vaccinated. I'm the only one in the class who doesn't have a vaccination record but I told him 'I DON'T WANT TO BE VACCINATED', so he sent me out again."

Mrs. Potter puts her arm around Sarah's shoulders and says, "You're completely right. You don't have to be vaccinated, if you and your parents don't want it. I'll take care of things. Tell your mother to call me."

When Sarah gets home again in the evening, she's still very upset. "I don't want to be vaccinated," she says over and over again.

Mom calls Mrs. Potter and thanks her for comforting Sarah so lovingly.

She then calls the school doctor. Mom is very angry and fuming. She asks the school doctor why he told Sarah that she had to be vaccinated. She also explains to him that she has a vaccine exemption for Sarah and had opted out of using vaccinations. After a long while, the telephone argument is over.

"He'll leave us alone now," she tells Sarah in an exhausted voice.

On Saturday, the time has finally come. The trip to Scout camp can begin.

The kids are all gathered in front of the school. Sarah is very excited. This will be the first time she'll be away from home for an entire week. She's also looking forward to telling stories late into the night with Laura, in their tent.

Their bags are loaded onto the bus and their bicycles go into the trailer. Sarah and Laura search quickly for a place where they can sit together for the whole trip.

Mom gives the troop leader the letter explaining that Sarah must not be vaccinated, just in case something should happen. At the end, everyone waves and the long anticipated trip can finally begin.

Scout camp is really wonderful. Laura and Sarah enjoy the many hours that they get to spend together. The best part is always sitting together around the campfire in the evening. Then, the troop leader plays wonderful songs on the guitar and they all get to sing along. It's so much fun that they forget the time and sit at the fire until sunset.

Every evening, one of the children gets to tell a spooky story. Sarah knows so many spooky stories from her grandma that she's asked to tell many scary stories in a row. Sarah is in the middle of telling the story about the wolf that lives in the forest and is sneaking up to the camp.

Suddenly, a rustling comes from Christian's tent. The kids stop talking and glance fearfully at the tent. There is something breathing loudly inside.

The kids cry out in fear, "The wolf! The wolf!"

The troop leader goes over bravely to the wiggling tent. Suddenly, everyone hears a loud yelp and something darts out of the tent. Laura begins to laugh and points at the creature: it's Max, the troop leader's dog. He's such a greedy fellow that he just ate Christian's chocolate. The kids laugh in relief and are glad that it wasn't a wolf, after all.

Three days before the end of camp, Laura suddenly gets sick. She has a fever and very red eyes. The troop leader immediately calls Laura's parents to come take her home.

A few hours later, Laura's mother arrives at the Scout camp and carries her ill daughter to the car. Sarah has tears in her eyes and is very sad. "It was so wonderful here with Laura," she tells Laura's mother, "and without her it's only half as much fun! Who will share my tent with me now?"

She waves sadly at Laura as they drive away and wipes away a few tears.

Laura also has tears in her eyes and is sad that the exciting trip is now over for her. On the other hand, she's happy that her Mommy is nearby again and can take care of her.

Sarah is a bit scared to sleep alone in her tent, because she is used to sharing it with Laura. They always told stories and giggled far into the night.

Sarah tells the troop leader that she doesn't want to sleep alone and he has a wonderful idea: "How would you feel about sharing a tent with Max, my dog?"

"Oh, that would be great! He can keep me warm and watch over me, and I can tell him scary stories because he never gets scared," Sarah answers excitedly.

Sarah spends the next few nights with Max. The two of them sleep snuggled close together. Max is so cuddly and warm that Sarah doesn't even need a sleeping bag.

After a week away, Sarah returns from Scout camp. Everyone has come to greet her. Even Grandma Helen is there. Sarah's parents are surprised to see Sarah get out of the bus without Laura.

"Laura got sick. She had a fever and had to be picked up after only four days," she tells them excitedly. "I have to go call her and ask how she's doing."

On the way home, Sarah's eyes sparkle as she tells them all about Scout camp. "I wasn't homesick at all," she says proudly. "It was just sad that Laura had to go, but I found a great replacement for the nights in my tent: Max, the troop leader's dog. He cuddled with me the whole time and watched over me. It was great!"

When Sarah gets home, she immediately calls her friend Laura.

Laura has been sick in bed for days. She has red spots all over and is still running a fever.

"I have measles," Laura tells Sarah, "the doctor was here today."

"How can that be? I thought you were vaccinated!" Sarah wonders.

"The doctor said that you can get measles, even if you're vaccinated against it," Laura explains to her.

"Huh? I don't get it. Why should you get vaccinated, if it doesn't even work?" Sarah asks with exasperation.

"I don't know," Laura answers.

"I'm sure my grandma can explain it to me. She knows everything," Sarah declares.

Later, Sarah, Tim and Grandma are sitting together in the living room. Sarah tells Grandma that Laura got measles despite being vaccinated. She still doesn't understand how that could have happened.

"You see?" Grandma says, "So it goes. Even when you're vaccinated, you're still not one hundred percent protected against getting an illness."

"But why should someone get vaccinated, if it doesn't even really protect them?" Sarah asks.

"Oh, my little one, I'll explain that to you later. You're still a bit young to understand how the health system works," Grandma replies with a heavy heart.

Tim runs to the kitchen and tears his picture down that he drew before Sarah went to Scout camp. He takes a marker and crosses out Laura's vaccination record. Grandma and Sarah laugh.

In the evening, Grandma puts the two children to bed and tells them another of her famous ghost stories from her days as a Girl Scout.

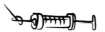

A Short Comment about Measles and its Vaccine

The Pathogen

The measles-pathogen is a Morbillivirus, which is passed on by droplet infection. Measles is a highly contagious disease. Today, over 95% of people over thirty have had the disease; due to vaccination, that number is much lower among the under fives: probably under 10%. (1)

The German Green Cross reports that nearly a third of all measles cases today involve adolescents or adults. At these ages, complications are twice as likely as for small children. Infants are also affected nowadays.

The Clinical Picture

After an incubation period of 10-14 days, an acute, infectious disease erupts with fever and catarrhal symptoms. On the 2nd or 3rd day, the typical measles rash begins to emerge, starting with the ears and then spreads to the face, torso and extremities. The eyes are puffy and inflamed and it looks as if the child had been crying the whole time. In addition, they show a pronounced sensitivity to light. The rash can last for 14 days before it begins to dissipate as fine flakes of skin. Patients are contagious during the incubation period and until the fever goes down. Known complications include middle ear infections, pneumonia, encephalitis and meningitis.

After measles infections, even years or decades later, a subacute, sclerosing panencephalitis or SSPE (a serious disease of the central nervous system) can emerge. However, since measles cases have become rare, the incidence of this disease is decreasing. The most problematic cases involve a measles infection within the first year of life (usually due to insufficient passive immunity from the mother). It has, however, been noted that the disease is more likely to occur in the vaccinated population (probably because most people are vaccinated) and the incubation period before the symptoms erupt is shorter. (2)

The incidence of measles encephalitis has been greatly reduced by vaccination programs (which was their main goal) but during the same period, the incidence of other types of encephalitis has increased. This increase has especially been observed with encephalitis that was caused by Varicella zoster, Enterovirus, HHV-6 (human herpes virus) and Chlamydia pneumonia. (3)

As the French chemist Pasteur said, "The pathogen is nothing, the terrain is everything." The other pathogens have simply filled in the space that was left by measles encephalitis. (4)

The biggest danger from vaccination is that of putting off the disease into adulthood and thereby increasing the risk of complications.

Back in the 60s, Dr. Bob C. Witsenburg was working in an African clinic and noticed that, paradoxically, the measles patients who recovered best were the ones who had had the highest fevers and the most pronounced rashes. When he thereupon left out the preventive medicines he had been using in half of his patients, the death rate plummeted from 35% to 7%.

Therapy

Doctors treat only the symptoms of measles. There is no known therapy to address the cause. In the case of secondary bacterial infections, the patient is given antibiotics.

Immunity

If one has had measles, one is immune for life. However, experts are coming to suspect that "wild boostering" (contact with wild measles viruses) may be necessary to maintain that life-long immunity. (5) That means that having no contact with measles carriers or patients can lead to a sufficient reduction in immunity to the point where, decades later, the disease could reoccur.

The Vaccine

Measles viruses for measles vaccines (MMR vaccines) are bred in cultures of embryonic chicken cells. For the measles vaccine, the viruses are weakened and antibiotics are applied. The remaining traces of chicken protein lead to the risk of an allergic reaction as a result of the vaccination.

Today, the vaccine usually takes the form of the MMR vaccine, which means it is given in combination with the vaccines for mumps and rubella, or in the MMRV form, which also contains a component of chicken pox. The MMR vaccine contains weakened, live viruses, which are given all at once. This is problematic, because one of the viruses can suppress the immune system, which can lead to the others causing insidious infections. (6)

The MMR vaccine also often contains two viruses from chicken cell cultures, which can trigger leukaemia in birds. Their possible effect on humans is unclear. (7)

The measles vaccination produces a short-term protective effect of 90-95% (BAG). Research has shown that, 1 year after vaccination, more than 16% of the people who were vaccinated no longer have immunity. (8)

This is the reason why some people are spreading propaganda that the age recommendation for the second MMR vaccination should be even younger than it is today and STIKO (German Standing Committee on Vaccination) is now also making this official recommendation. It is however questionable whether even such measures will solve this dilemma because a number of studies have shown that, although the booster vaccination leads to another increase of antibodies, they once again fall away sharply so that no lasting immunity remains. (9)

In the USA and Gambia, two countries with the highest vaccination rates against measles, there have been regular epidemics of measles, often with very serious progressions of the disease. In addition, because the proportion of adults who catch measles is greater nowadays, the rate of complications has increased (although their absolute number has declined).

Because of the reduction in actual immunity to measles and the more seldom contact with wild viruses, mothers who were vaccinated against measles can provide their children with only a weak passive immunity. It used to be (before measles vaccines) that measles cases among infants were the exception to the rule, but the proportion of infants who catch measles now has increased (although the absolute number has declined). According to Gold, in 1995, half of the 300 recorded measles cases in the USA involved infants and adults. (10)

RSV Infections

For many years now, Germany has seen an increase in serious respiratory infections with RS viruses (RSV = respiratory syncitial virus), especially among children under 2 years of age. It is suspected that there is a connection between the introduction of the measles vaccine (in Germany since 1973), which was given to most of today's mothers back then, and today's increase in susceptibility of children to the RS virus. This supposition is supported by the fact that both the measles virus and the RS virus belong to the same Paramyxoviridae family. The study furthermore states that in countries with a low percentage of measles vaccination, there seem to be fewer cases of serious respiratory infections in children who require treatment in a clinic. Similar developments have been observed in the USA, Great Britain and Sweden. (11)

Of the first infections (by the end of their 2nd year of life, nearly 100% of children have had an RSV infection) around 2% have symptoms severe enough to require hospitalization. (12) Among the hospitalized cases, the death rate is around 1.7%.

About 5% of infected children develop a pseudo-croup (13) and an RSV infection is seen as a risk factor for SIDS (sudden infant death syndrome). (14)

In other words, in Germany alone, that comes to around 15,000 hospitalizations of children and around 250 deaths. This reality has been strengthened by the widespread implementation of measles vaccination.

The Absence of Wild Boostering

Vaccination against measles has led to a sharp reduction in circulating wild viruses. Before the days of vaccination, these used to maintain a person's immunity through unnoticed contacts. As a result of their absence, the age at which people are catching measles is older. Older adults often no longer have sufficient immunity to measles. Levy from Johns Hopkins University comes to the conclusion that, if there were a measles epidemic in the year 2050, there could be over 25,000 deaths. The option should therefore be carefully considered of limiting future vaccination to risk groups. This, in turn, might restore the previous, ecological balance between the virus and the human population. (15)

The Problem of Mass Vaccination

As suggested above, the measles vaccine provides only a short protective effect. Even if we were to vaccinate 95% of the population twice, somewhere around ten per cent of children born every year would reach adulthood with no protection. This comes to around 70,000 adults for every birth year in Germany, and around 7,000 in Switzerland, who, one might say, are sitting on a ticking time bomb. In comparison to that, before vaccination efforts, 99% of people had had measles by the time they were fifteen and had thus acquired a lifelong immunity to another measles episode. In the long term, it is impossible through vaccination to protect the population against measles.

Indeed, such a goal would require vaccinating the entire population and, to compensate for the lack of wild boostering, regular booster shots would be necessary, since the risk of the virus being brought in from outside the country would remain.

Virologists at the University of Bonn recently identified bats as a natural reservoir for pathogens including, among others, measles and mumps. This proves that the goal of the WHO to use vaccination to eradicate measles from around the world is absurd. (16)

Measles Extermination is Impossible, Despite High Vaccination Rates: China Case Study

In China, a country in which measles vaccination is required by law, there are high rates of vaccination and yet there are still measles outbreaks. For example, in Zhejiang Province, measles, mumps and rubella are common, although over 99% of the people there are vaccinated. (17)

The Bulletin of the World Health Organization also published a study regarding the most recent measles outbreaks in all of China. Between 2005 and October of 2013, 596,391 measles infections were reported in China, which led to 368 measles-related deaths. From 2009 to 2012, there were 707 outbreaks of measles. In 2013, there were notably more. The average age sank from 83 months in 2005 to 14 months in 2012 and 11 months between January and October of 2013. This proves that the vaccination program is not only not very effective, but also is leading to a reduction in the age of infection to under a year of age, which drastically increases the risk of complications. (18)

Side Effects, Vaccination Complications and Vaccine-Related Injuries Regarding Measles

Aside from local reactions at the puncture site, vaccinations can result in fever, symptoms that resemble measles, middle ear infections, thrombocytopaenia and, among people with chicken or egg allergies, also allergic reactions. Autoimmune diseases, neurological disorders and incidence of diabetes mellitus (as noted in the patient information leaflet of the American MMR vaccine) have also been observed after measles vaccination. More recently, a connection with the incidence of autism has been observed and discussed (regarding the MMR vaccine).

Encephalitis after a Measles Vaccination

Encephalitis, in this case vaccination encephalitis, is also a known complication that can occur after a measles vaccination. The research group Weibel, Caserta, Benor and Evans report about a number of children in their study, who developed encephalitis after their measles vaccinations and sustained lasting brain damage as a result (or even died).

Vaccination encephalitis often progresses without pronounced symptoms, which leads to it being underreported as a vaccine complication. There may therefore very well be yet more cases. (19) In children, encephalitis can lead to developmental problems, which may not yet be noticeable at the time of the vaccination.

Autism or Chronic Inflammation of the Intestines after a Measles Vaccination

For some time now, there has been a controversial discussion about the connection between the MMR vaccination and the incidence of autism and of illnesses such as Crohn's Disease. This began with the research team of A. J. Wakefield. Wakefield called the disease he observed after the MMR vaccination "autistic enterocolitis." In England, this led to a drastic reduction in vaccination rates.

The incidence of autism has increased dramatically since the eighties, especially in children in their second year of life. "The rates of autism have escalated dramatically. What used to be considered a rare disorder has become a near-epidemic," according to Dan Burton, the Chairman of the 2000 House Gov. Reform Committee on Autism and Childhood Vaccines. (20)

Wakefield and others point out that the MMR vaccination can lead to a chain of cause and effect between the vaccine viruses and the immune system, which can lead to inflammation of nerves or nerve damage. Among children with autism, one often finds elevated levels of antibodies against the myelin sheath (the fatty, protective covering of the nerves) and also elevated levels of measles antibodies. Wakefield suggests that there may be a connection between these two observations in which the vaccine viruses could have a causal effect. (21)

Conclusion

If treated properly (no fever reducers, no antibiotics to prevent secondary infections and supplementation with Vitamin A), measles is a harmless children's disease. Even into the '70s, measles was treated as a normal illness which every child went through. It was not until many vaccines were introduced and the WHO made a goal of exterminating it that measles was degraded to being a boogyman. The unjustified panic-mongering in the media serves only the goal of making the population feel insecure and instilling the view in people that vaccination is the moral choice. Measles returns in regular waves and thus the current outbreak (2014/2015) in Berlin is simply one of these waves.

The argument that is meant to convince everyone to get vaccinated is the information about how dangerous measles is. The RKI (Robert Koch Institute) reports, "According to the literature, out of every 10,000 to 20,000 cases of the measles, one leads to death. According to the Statistisches Bundesamt, death cause statistics reveal that, since the year 2000, there were 1-2 measles-related death cases per year (with one exception: in 2007, no death case was registered)." (22)

The Robert Koch Institute draws from that, "This is equivalent to a rate of 1 death per 1,000 measles cases." (23) It should be noted that such an incidence is much too low for a death count statistic to come to any reliable conclusion. Furthermore, in these calculation games, there was no attempt made to account for the unreported measles cases.

This discussion would not be complete without noting that the database of the PEI Institute has recorded roughly the same number of deaths after the measles vaccination. In other words, according to official records, there is roughly one death per year after a measles vaccination. This does not draw into account the unknown cases in which the measles vaccine was not seen as the proximate cause of death (which comes to more than 90%). It also fails to mention the other side effects after MMR vaccinations, which are downplayed during the discussion (these reports are also based on the official numbers and thereby leave out the unreported cases).

About the authors:

Andreas Bachmair is a classical homeopath with a practice in Kreuzlingen by the Bodensee in Switzerland. The focus of his work for over ten years has been the treatment of vaccine-related injuries. This led him to create the website www.impfschaden.info to educate people about the dangers of vaccination. Seven years ago, impfschaden.info was translated into English and can be accessed at www.vaccineinjury.info. With nearly 20,000 participants so far, one of the largest studies to document the health of unvaccinated children is currently underway on those two websites. He is the author and publisher of several books critical of vaccinations, "Vaccine-Free", "Leitfaden zur Impfentscheidung" and "Risiko und Nebenwirkung Impfschaden". The latter two are unfortunately not yet available in English.

Madlen Maker is from Berlin and has lived in Switzerland for many years. After her degree in food technology, she decided to change directions and now works as a phytotherapist, nutritional adviser and manual therapist.

About the illustrator:

Alena Ryazanowa is a professional artist, painter and sculptor from Irkutsk in Siberia. Her cartoons and drawings are well-known in her home country. Her sculptures decorate the streets of Irkutsk and can be found in many businesses in her city. She illustrates books and magazines and has collaborated with Andreas Bachmair for many years. Their first project together was the book "Leben ohne Impfung", illustrated with her enchanting caricatures.

About the editor:

Helen Kimball-Brooke is a semi-retired professional homeopath living in London, UK. She was born, raised and educated to university level in New England, USA, then studied Translation (French, Italian, English) in Paris, France, where she worked for many years as both an in-house and freelance translator and technical writer. She and her British husband have two healthy grown-up daughters who are only partially vaccinated and a very healthy totally unvaccinated black Labrador dog. Helen has been an active member of EFVV, the European Forum for Vaccine Vigilance, since 2002, and has been a member of the Board since 2012.

Literary Sources:

1. Impfen: Routine oder Individualisation Eine Standortbestimmung aus hausärztlicher Sicht, 2. Auflage 2000, Arbeitsgruppe für differnenzierte Impfungen, S. 32

2. Dyken PR, Cunningham SC, Ward LC.: Changing character of subacute sclerosing panencephalitis in the United States.Pediatr Neurol. 1991 Mar-Apr;7(2):151./Dyken PR: Neuroprogressive disease of post-infectious origin: a review of a resurging subacute sclerosing panencephalitis (SSPE).,Ment Retard Dev Disabil Res Rev 2001;7(3):217-25

3. Koskiniemi M, Korppi M, Mustonen K, Rantala H, Muttilainen M, Herrgard E, Ukkonen P, Vaheri A. : Epidemiology of encephalitis in children. A prospective multicentre study. Eur J Pediatr. 1997 Jul;156(7):541-5.

4. Martin Hirte: Impfen: pro und contra . S. 187

5. Impfen, Routine oder Individualisation, Arbeitsgruppe für differenzierte Impfungen2 Aufl. März 2000, S. 32

6. Halsey,-N-A: Increased mortality after high titer measles vaccines: too much of a good thing.Pediatr-Infect-Dis-J. 1993 Jun; 12(6): 462-5

7. Tsang et al, J Virol, July 1999, 73(7): 5843-5851

8. Mitchell LA, Tingle AJ, Decarie D, Lajeunesse C.: Serologic responses to measles, mumps, and rubella (MMR) vaccine in healthy infants: failure to respond to measles and mumps components may influence decisions on timing of the second dose of MMR.Can J Public Health. 1998 Sep-Oct;89(5):325-8

9. Bartoloni A, Cutts FT, Guglielmetti P, Brown D, Bianchi Bandinelli ML, Hurtado H, Roselli M.:Response to measles revaccination among Bolivian school-aged children Trans R Soc Trop Med Hyg. 1997 Nov-Dec;91(6):716-8.

10. Gold, E. : Current progress in measles eradication in the United states; Infect Med 1997, 14(4) 297-300

11. Weigl A, Puppe W, Belke O, Neususs J, Bagci F, Schmitt HJ., The descriptive epidemiology of severe lower respiratory tract infections in children in Kiel, Germany, Klin Padiatr. 2005 Sep-Oct;217(5):259-67.)

12. Christian P. Speer, Manfred Gahr: Pädiatrie. 2. Auflage. Springer, Heidelberg/ Berlin 2005, ISBN 3-540-20791-0.

13. Respiratory Syncytial Virus. In: Pschyrembel. 262. Auflage. De Gruyter, Berlin/ Boston, Mass. 2010, ISBN 978-3-11-021152-8.

14. Pädiatrie. In: Hanns Ackermann: ALLEX - alles fürs Examen : das Kompendium für die 2. ÄP. Band B: Klinische Fächer. Thieme, Stuttgart/ New York (NY) 2012, S. 590

15. lit. H.U. Albonico "Gewaltige Medizin", Tagblatt, 6.7.02 "Viele Fragen sind unbeantwortet"-Masern wegen Impfverweigerung

16. Drexler F. Nature Communications 3, Article number:796; doi:10.1038/ncomms1796; www.nature.com

17. Zhifang Wang, Rui Yan, Hanqing He, Qian Li, Guohua Chen, Shengxu Yang, and Enfu Chen: Difficulties in Eliminating Measles and Controlling Rubella and Mumps: A Cross-Sectional Study of a First Measles and Rubella Vaccination and a Second Measles, Mumps, and Rubella Vaccination, PLoS One. 2014; 9(2): e89361; http://www.ncbi.nlm.nih.gov/pmc/articles/PMC3930734

18. Chao Ma, Lixin Hao, Yan Zhang, Qiru Su, Lance Rodewald, Zhijie An, Wenzhou Yu, Jing Ma, Ning Wen, Huiling Wang, Xiaofeng Liang, Huaqing Wang, Weizhong Yang, Li Li, and Huiming Luo: Monitoring progress towards the elimination of measles in China: an analysis of measles surveillance data, Bull World Health Organ. May 1, 2014; 92(5): 340–347; http://www.ncbi.nlm.nih.gov/pmc/articles/PMC4007128/

19. Martinon-Torres F, Magarinos MM, Picon M, Fernandez-Seara MJ, Rodriguez-Nunez A, Martinon-Sanchez JM. R: Self-limited acute encephalopathy related to measles component of viral triple vaccineRev Neurol. 1999 May 1-15;28(9):881-2.

20. Chairman Burton: Government Reform Committee to Hold Hearing on the Rise of Autism; What: Government Reform Committee hearing: "Autism: Present Challenges, Future Needs - Why the Increased Rates?" Thursday, April 6, 1999 at 10:30 a.m.

21. Wakefield et al, Inflammatory Bowel Disease Study Group at the Royal Free Hospital, London, Ileal Lymphoid Nodular Hyperplasia, Non-Specific Colitis and Pervasive Developmental Disorder in Children, Lancet, 28th February 1998

Eggers, Autistic Syndrome (Kanners) and Vaccination Against Smallpox, Klinical Paediatrics, 1st March 1976 (944354 PubMed, 76172565 Medline)

Weizman, Weizman, Szekely, Livni and Wijsenbeek, published in the American Journal of Psychiatry 1982 Nov 139 (11) 1462-5

Dr. H. Fudenburg, Dialysable Lymphocyte Extract In Infantile Onset Autism: A Pilot Study, has been published (date/journal not identified), NeuroImmuno-Therapeutics Research Foundation, 1092 Boiling Springs Road, Spartanburg, South Carolina (fax 803 591 0622)

Dr. Vijendra Singh, College of Pharmacy, University of Michigan, Ann Arbor, joint with the late Professor Reed Warren, Professor of Biology, Centre for Persons with Disabilities, Utah State University in Logan and Adjunct Professor of Psychiatry, University of Utah, and also Dennis Odell, published in Brain Behaviour, March 1993

Anne-Marie Plesner, Department of Epidemiology, Statens Seruminstitut, Copenhagen, Lancet, Vol 345, Feb 4th 1995

Montgomery, Morris, Pounder and Wakefield, Inflammatory Bowel Disease Study Group, Dept. Of Medicine, Royal Free Hospital, London, Paramyxovirus Infections in Childhood and Subsequent Inflammatory Bowel Disease (https://web.archive.org/web/20140424142823/

Singh and Yang, Department of Biology and Biotechnology Center, Utah State University, University of Michigan College of Pharmacy, published Clinical Immunology and Immunopathology, October 1998

Bitnun et al, Measles Inclusion-Body Encephalitis Caused By the Vaccine Strain of Measles Virus, Clinical Infectious Diseases Journal, 1999; 29 855-61, (October)

Paper Presented to US Congressional Oversight Committee on Autism and Immunisation, Professor John O'Leary, Dublin Womens Hospital, April 2000)

22. http://www.rki.de/DE/Content/Infekt/EpidBull/Merkblaetter/Ratgeber_Masern.html

23. http://www.rki.de/DE/Content/Infekt/EpidBull/Merkblaetter/Ratgeber_Masern.html#doc2374536bodyText7

Made in the USA
Coppell, TX
18 July 2020